Knuffle Bunny Too

A Case of Mistaken Identity

This book is dedicated to
preschool students everywhere

ISBN-13: 978-0-545-10355-8
ISBN-10: 0-545-10355-X

12 11 10 9 8 7 6 5 4 3 2 1   8 9 10 11 12 13/0

Printed in the U.S.A.   08

First Scholastic printing, September 2008

The images in this book are a melding of hand-drawn ink sketches and
photography. The sketches were colored and shaded digitally; the
photographs were taken in Park Slope, Brooklyn, and altered to expunge
sundry urban debris and protect the innocent. The photographs are the
author's (the Grand Army Plaza panorama required the additional skills
and enthusiasm of Mr. Tom Drysdale).

KNUFFLE BUNNY TOO

A CASE OF MISTAKEN IDENTITY BY Mo Willems

SCHOLASTIC INC.

New York   Toronto   London   Auckland   Sydney
Mexico City   New Delhi   Hong Kong   Buenos Aires

One morning, not so long ago,
Trixie took a walk with her daddy.

By now, Trixie really
knew how to talk.

959
Guess what I'm going to do. I'm going to show Amy, and then I'll show Meg, and…

...then I'll show Margot, and then I'll show Jane, and then I'll show Leela, and then I'll show Rebecca, and then I'll show Noah, and then I'll show Robbie, and then I'll show Toshi, and then I'll show Casey, and then I'll show Conny, and then I'll show Parker, and then I'll show Brian, and then ...

And talk, and talk.

Trixie was excited because she was taking her one-of-a-kind Knuffle Bunny someplace very special . . .

school!

Trixie couldn't wait to show Knuffle Bunny to Ms. Greengrove and all her friends in Pre-K.

But just as her daddy
kissed her good-bye,
Trixie saw Sonja.

Suddenly, Trixie's one-of-a-kind
Knuffle Bunny wasn't so
one-of-a-kind anymore.

The morning did not go well.

The afternoon was worse.

When the school bell rang, Ms. Greengrove returned the Knuffle Bunnies.

And the day got better.

Then, before she knew it,

it was time to go home.

Trixie "ate" her dinner,

devoured her
dessert,

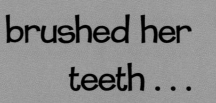

brushed her
teeth . . .

and tried to escape the Mommy and Daddy robots from planet Snurp!

At half-past bedtime, Trixie was tucked in,

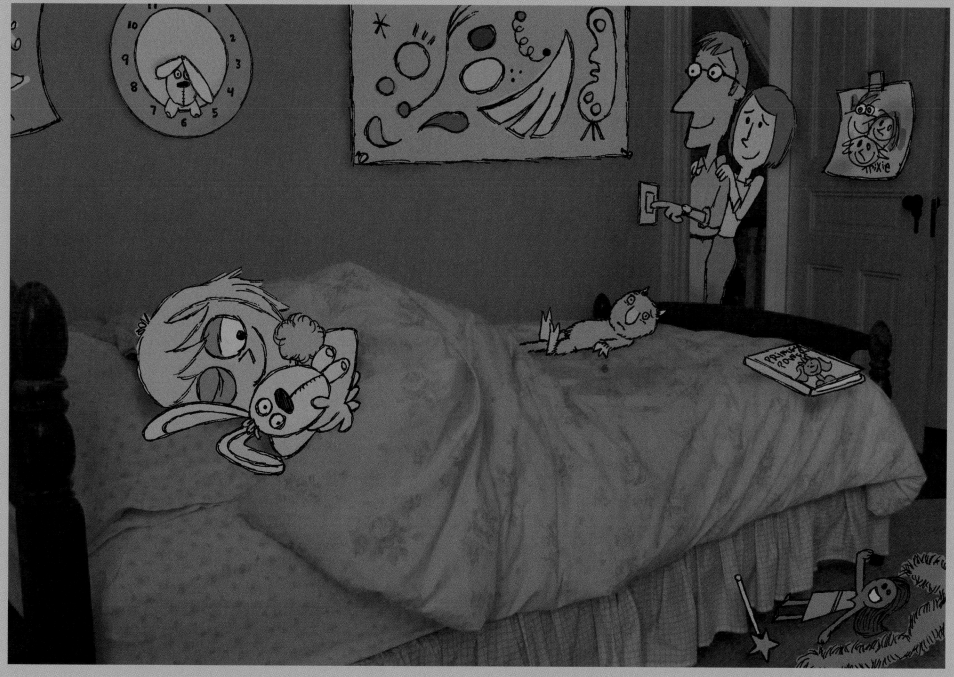

ready for sleep.

But a few hours later . . .

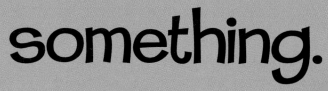

Trixie marched into her
mommy and daddy's
room and said:

Trixie's daddy tried to explain what "2:30 a.m." means.

He asked, "Can we deal with this in the morning?"

Trixie's daddy went to the phone.

Before he even made it
down the stairs,

the phone rang.

said a man's voice on the other end.

replied Trixie's daddy.

Arrangements were made.

Trixie and her daddy rushed
across the neighborhood!

Trixie did not
want to be late.

There was an exchange.

And the Knuffle Bunnies were back

where they belonged.

said Sonja.

Trixie replied.

Then they both said,

I'm glad you
got your
bunny back!

at the **exact**

same

time!

And that is how Trixie found her first* best friend.

*Knuffle Bunny excepted, of course.

Special thanks to the real Trixie and her mommy, Tom Drysdale, the Brooklyn Public Library, the Robinson family, the Lewine family, Ms. Theope, Ms. Holton, and the PS107 community.

EPILOGUE

The next morning, both Trixie and Sonja rushed to school.

The new best friends had a lot of catching up to do.